# AWESOME AMBULANCES

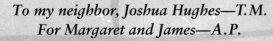

*To my neighbor, Joshua Hughes—T.M.*
*For Margaret and James—A.P.*

KINGFISHER
LONDON & NEW YORK

Text copyright © Tony Mitton 2018
Illustrations copyright © Ant Parker 2018
Designed by Anthony Hannant (LittleRedAnt) 2018
Published in the United States by Kingfisher,
175 Fifth Ave., New York, NY 10010
Kingfisher is an imprint of Macmillan Children's Books, London.

Distributed in the U.S. and Canada by Macmillan, 175 Fifth Ave., New York, NY 10010

Library of Congress Cataloging-in-Publication data have been applied for.

ISBN 978-0-7534-7457-0 (HB)
ISBN 978-0-7534-7458-7 (PB)

Kingfisher books are available for special promotions and premiums. For details contact:
Special Markets Department, Macmillan, 175 Fifth Ave., New York, NY 10010.

For more information, please visit
www.kingfisherbooks.com

Printed in China
9 8 7 6 5 4 3 2 1

# AWESOME AMBULANCES

Tony Mitton and
Ant Parker

KINGFISHER
LONDON & NEW YORK

If you've had an accident,
or if you're very sick,
an ambulance assists you.
Its response is very quick.

When the station takes a call
to say that you're in need,
an ambulance will get to you
by driving at great speed.

To clear the road ahead of it,
its siren fills the air.
It tells the other drivers
someone's hurt or needing care.

For extra visibility,
especially at night,
an ambulance on call will flash
its very vivid lights.

To operate an ambulance
there has to be a crew.
They're highly trained. These paramedics
know just what to do.

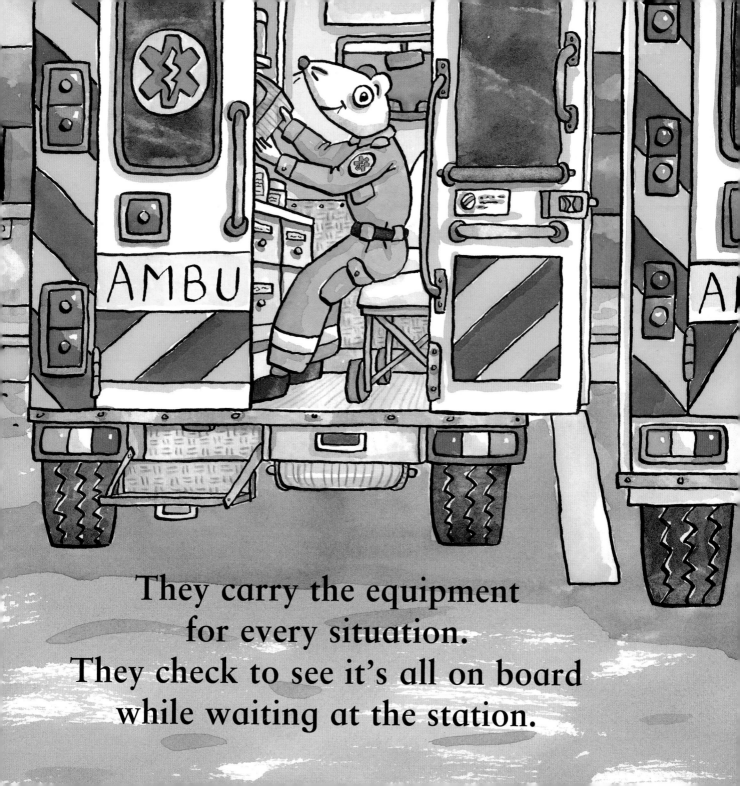

They carry the equipment
for every situation.
They check to see it's all on board
while waiting at the station.

They store all kinds of bandages,
in case you start to bleed.

AIRWAYS

SYRINGES

To deal with pain and problems,
they've medicine you might need.

There's oxygen to help you breathe,
if you're really sick.

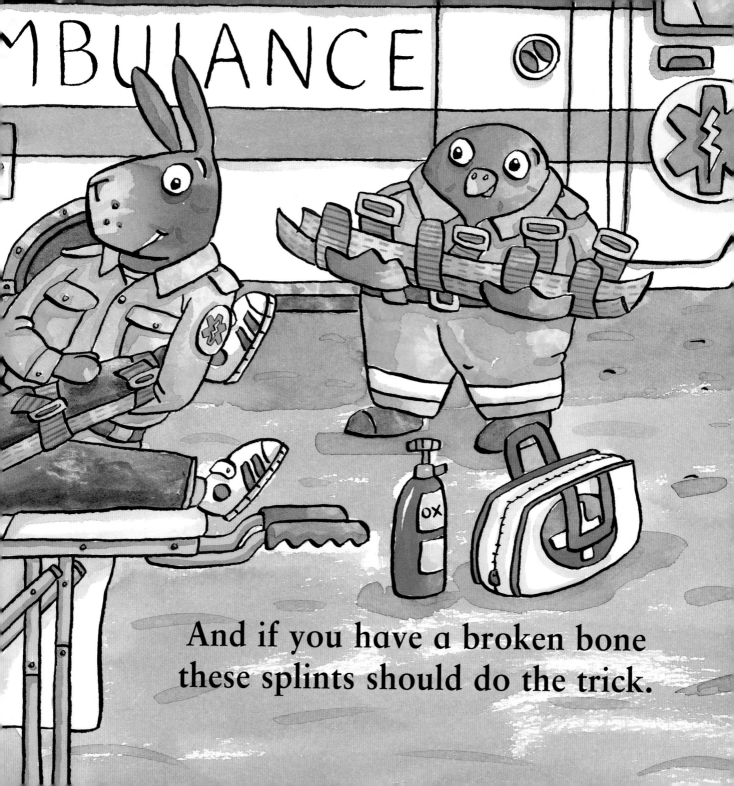

And if you have a broken bone
these splints should do the trick.

For people who are very weak
and cannot move or stand,
the paramedics use a bed on wheels
to lend a hand.

This bed is called a stretcher.
It gives a gentle ride.
And after that it's folded up
and packed away inside.

When the patient's safely in
the ambulance at last
it's time to get them treated
at the hospital—and fast!

The driver travels speedily,
but keeps the vehicle steady.
The hospital is radioed
to have them at the ready.

On the way the paramedics
use their skill and care
to keep the patient comfortable
until arriving there.

Once they're at the hospital
the staff are there to meet them.

They quickly take the patient off
to doctors who will treat them.

Back at base the paramedics
clean and check the stock.

Hooray for Awesome Ambulances
ready round the clock!

# Ambulance bits

## First aid kit
this carries equipment for many emergency situations

## Collapsible stretcher
this is used to move patients who are too hurt or sick to walk

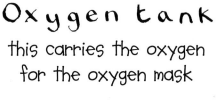

## Oxygen tank
this carries the oxygen for the oxygen mask

## Disposable gloves
these keep the paramedics' hands free from germs and infection

## Splint
this will keep a broken arm or leg straight until it can be treated

## Oxygen mask
this gives oxygen to patients when they're not breathing properly

## Bandaids
these patch up very small cuts or wounds

## Bandages
these are used to cover wounds

## Oxymeter
this measures how much oxygen is in a person's blood

## Collect all the AMAZING MACHINES books by Tony Mitton and Ant Parker!

   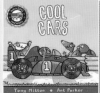   

HC ISBN 978-0-7534-7457-0
TP ISBN 978-0-7534-7458-7
BB ISBN 978-0-7534-7494-5

HC ISBN 978-0-7534-5403-9
TP ISBN 978-0-7534-5915-7
BB ISBN 978-0-7534-7370-2

TP ISBN 978-0-7534-5916-4
BB ISBN 978-0-7534-7416-7

HC ISBN 978-0-7534-5802-0
TP ISBN 978-0-7534-7207-1
BB ISBN 978-0-7534-7395-5

TP ISBN 978-0-7534-5304-9
BB ISBN 978-0-7534-7394-8

TP ISBN 978-0-7534-5307-0
BB ISBN 978-0-7534-7373-3

HC ISBN 978-0-7534-7290-3
TP ISBN 978-0-7534-7291-0
BB ISBN 978-0-7534-7418-1

HC ISBN 978-0-7534-7292-7
TP ISBN 978-0-7534-7293-4
BB ISBN 978-0-7534-7419-8

HC ISBN 978-0-7534-7455-6
TP ISBN 978-0-7534-7456-3
BB ISBN 978-0-7534-7495-2

TP ISBN 978-0-7534-5305-6
BB ISBN 978-0-7534-7371-9

TP ISBN 978-0-7534-7208-8
BB ISBN 978-0-7534-7417-4

TP ISBN 978-0-7534-5306-3
BB ISBN 978-0-7534-7372-6

TP ISBN 978-0-7534-5917-1
BB ISBN 978-0-7534-7397-9

TP ISBN 978-0-7534-5918-8
BB ISBN 978-0-7534-7396-2

## Younger children will love these AMAZING MACHINES tabbed board books:

ISBN 978-0-7534-7440-2

ISBN 978-0-7534-7439-6

## Listen out for the sound book— with 10 airplane sounds!

ISBN 978-0-7534-7328-3

## Get busy with the AMAZING MACHINES activity books— with a model to make and stickers!

   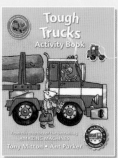

ISBN 978-0-7534-7255-2

ISBN 978-0-7534-7256-9

ISBN 978-0-7534-7257-6

ISBN 978-0-7534-7254-5